SHOCK SHOP

Long Lost

Jan Mark

Illustrated by David Roberts

MACMILLAN CHILDREN'S BOOKS

First published 2002 by Macmillan Children's Books

This edition published 2002 by Macmillan Children's Books
a division of Macmillan Publishers Limited
20 New Wharf Road, London N1 9RR
Basingstoke and Oxford
www.panmacmillan.com

Associated companies throughout the world

ISBN 0 330 39749 4

1 3 5 7 9 8 6 4 2

A CIP catalogue record for this book is available from
the British Library.

Typeset by Intype London Ltd
Printed and bound in Great Britain by Mackays of Chatham plc, Kent

Chapter 1

It was dark at the top of the stairs and dark halfway up where the staircase went round the corner, doubling back on itself like a hairpin. The lamp burned low in the hall downstairs because they had to save gas, and the one on the landing burned even lower. Neither light could quite reach that place in the middle, the hinge of the hairpin, or the locked door of the room they no longer used because of the damp.

The door stood back from the wall in a little alcove, dim by day and deeply dark by night – a kind of solid, standing darkness that might detach itself from the alcove and spring out at anyone who went by, to cling, and follow, up or down.

There were thirteen stairs on the first flight and seven on the second. George had found a way to get past the dark in the middle by going up at a run. Then he gripped the newel post, leaped from the twelfth stair and swung

himself round, up, on to the next flight, without setting foot on the half landing. Convinced that for those two airborne seconds he was moving at thirty miles an hour at least – as fast as a *train* – he knew that nothing could get him.

"Aren't you getting a little old for this, Georgie?" Mother asked him, lured out of the sitting-room by the thuds of his take-off and descent. Coming down was faster and even louder.

If only he had a lantern. Then, reading the *Boys' Own Paper*, George came across an article, with diagrams, on heliography – a way of sending messages with mirrors and sunlight. There was no sun in the hall but, experimenting with a bit of glass under the gas bracket at the foot of the stairs, he found he could flash a disc of light into the alcove – up, down, across. Nothing there. He still went past it quickly but: "Nothing there. I've proved it."

That was before he met Bertram.

"Just because you can't see anything," Bertram said, with his light and idle smile, "it doesn't mean that there isn't anything to see."

But the evening that George first tried out his heliograph, Bertram Bassett-Milne was still long lost.

George was half an orphan. However bad things became – and they were often very bad – George clung to that half. Whole orphans were poor, sad things who came from a special place, an orphanage. George and Elsie still had their mother. Father had died so long ago that George could not even remember what he had looked like. There were photographs on the piano, of a jolly-looking man with  a neat beard and a cheerful moustache, but George had been so small when Father died that all he could recall were shiny boots and a long, dark greatcoat; not the face above it, not even the beard.

Elsie, who was older, could remember, but

she did not like talking about Father, and Mother still cried sometimes when he was mentioned, so George had learned to avoid the subject. Elsie had been studying music at the time, planning one day to go to the Royal Academy, but there was no money for that these days. Elsie had to earn a living and now taught music herself, at a girls' school in Highgate.

"I'm a bad teacher," she said angrily, "but it doesn't matter. A good teacher would be wasted on those dull little beasts."

"They can't *all* be dull," George suggested. He knew about school only from books and the *Boys' Own Paper* and thought it must be thrilling all day long.

"Oh, can't they *just*?" Elsie snapped. "Dull and stupid. They only go to The Manor because nowhere else will take them. And nowhere else would employ *me* to teach them."

George did lessons with the Vicar. Elsie

refused to teach him and George was grateful for that.

Elsie did not want to be employed at all. She longed for the concerts and evenings at the theatre, dances and parties, boating trips and lawn tennis games that she had grown up to expect, that had all vanished away when Father died. George had never had the chance to expect anything at all. He certainly did not expect things to change.

Elsie was at home when the letter came. It was an official-looking thing in a long envelope and the postman had to knock because it was too large to go through the letter box, and too impressively stiff to fold. George took it in to Mother at the breakfast table and stood by to watch her open it.

Mother stared and turned the envelope in her fingers, too nervous to slit it open. Letters like that had arrived before, from lawyers, and they never brought good news.

In the end, Elsie leaned across the table and

took it gently from Mother's shaking hands.

"Let me," she said bravely, and stabbed the paper knife under the flap. Then, in the bold impatient way she did everything, she drew out the folded paper inside, opened it and began to read, silently. If there was going to be bad news she wanted to let it out a bit at a time.

George and Mother watched her, gripping each other's hands. Elsie's eyes were growing wider and wider; her mouth fell open, her faced turned pale, then pink.

"What *is* it?" Mother said desperately. "What's happened?"

Elsie could not speak. She passed the

letter across the table and George, reading over Mother's shoulder, learned what had happened.

The letter was from a firm of lawyers – Garbutt, Garbutt, Garbutt and Troon – writing to tell them that Brigadier-General Sir Gervase Bassett-Milne, Bart., had sadly died in Jamaica, six months ago, and that Mother was one of his heirs and assigns. Mr Garbutt, *one* of the Mr Garbutts, looked forward to meeting her at her earliest convenience.

"What's an heir and assign?" George wanted to know.

"It means we've inherited something in a will," Elsie said. "Father must have been the heir. I suppose Mother is his assign, now he's dead. *One* of the heirs and assigns, it says. Oh well, ten to one there are dozens of them and we'll get sixpence and a cast-iron bedstead."

"Sir Gervase Bassett-Milne *Bart*?"

"That means Baronet," Mother said.

"Is he a lord?" Who would have thought they had lords in the family.

"Sort of," Elsie said, "but not one of the best sort. Nothing like so grand as an earl or a marquess."

George had recently read a book called *Little Lord Fauntleroy* in which a fatherless American boy discovered that he would be an earl when he grew up. Was that going to happen to him?

"Not likely," Elsie said. "We must be second cousins, five times removed and once again to make sure. Anyway, they're Bassett-Milnes. We're mere Bassetts."

Mother went into London two days later to meet the Mr Garbutts and Troon. She took the bus to the station, but came home in a cab with a box of cakes for tea.

"There," said Elsie, peering through the

9

curtains. "That's the end of our inheritance. She has blown the lot on high-class confectionery."

But Elsie was wrong, for once. Sir Gervase had been Father's long-lost great-uncle who had managed to quarrel with every single member of his family except Father and Grandfather, who had both died before Sir Gervase went on the warpath. Bit by bit, Mr Garbutt had told Mother, Sir Gervase had cut one relative after another out of his will until there were only three or four left. One of them had been Father.

"But how can he inherit anything if he's dead?" George asked.

"We are his heirs and assigns," Mother said. "We get your father's share because he left everything to me." Not, they all thought silently, that he had been able to leave very much.

"What about the title?" Elsie said. "Don't tell me our Georgie-Porgie is going to be *Sir*

George, the ninety-fifth Baronet. Oh, my eye!"

"Don't be vulgar," Mother said. "I'm sure you don't speak to the girls like that."

"Not in their hearing," Elsie said.

"Sir Gervase couldn't choose who got the title. It goes to his grandson, Sir Gilbert Bassett-Milne. He's the eighth Baronet, Elsie."

"And has Sir Gilbert inherited any cash – or did he get cut out too?" Elsie said.

"I didn't ask," Mother said. "It would have been indelicate."

"I *don't* think," Elsie said.

George could think of only one thing.

"How much has he left us?"

Mother said slowly, "Twenty thousand pounds," and, for once, even Elsie had nothing to say.

That evening they sat in the parlour and talked about how different life was going to be. It had started to be different already. Elsie had recklessly piled coals on the fire and it roared up the chimney instead of smouldering sulkily while they huddled around it, shivering.

"Shall we get the builders in?" George asked.

The builders had been a dream for years, almost mythical, like Father Christmas or fairy godmothers. Now they could mend the roof, put in new windows, stop the damp in the room on the stairs . . .

"We could *move*," said Elsie. "A decent address, at last."

"You won't have to go back to The Manor in April," George said.

"No, I can try for the Academy instead, can't I, Mother? And George can go to school. Lucky George. Where shall we send him – Eton, Harrow? Gas Street Board School?"

"Before we do anything else I must see our

12

own Mr Cousins and take advice about investments – *sound* investments," Mother said. "If only your poor dear father . . ."

"I think we *should* move," Elsie persisted. "As soon as possible. We're suddenly going to discover a lot of long-lost relations – or rather, the long-lost relations are going to discover our money."

"Don't be silly, darling," Mother said. "We aren't going to do anything yet." But that night she turned up the gas in the hall and on the landing. The whole staircase was lit from the top to the bottom and there were no shadows around the door on the hairpin bend.

George went very slowly up to bed thinking, *We're going to be rich*.

Mother had said, "No, not rich, comfortable. If I invest wisely."

George could not see the difference himself, but he realized what Elsie had meant about the long-lost relatives – all those people who had abandoned them to struggle on alone

after Father died, leaving only his unwise
investments.

Everyone would want to know them now.

Chapter 2

Many letters began to arrive, congratulating Mother on her wonderful fortune and containing tactful suggestions about how much *good* she could do with it.

"Charity begins at home," Elsie said to George, knowing how tender-hearted Mother was. To Mother she said, "You haven't got time to deal with all these, let me answer them." She collected the post every morning and spent an hour in her room writing tactful but hard-hearted replies. She had bought a beautiful new fountain pen and some handsome writing paper to do it with.

"Because one is being ruthless one need not

be stingy with it," Elsie said elegantly, and sitting at the piano accompanied herself in a little song she had composed.

> "Elsie Bassett,
> Worth a mint,
> Nib of gold
> And heart of flint."

One day an intriguing letter arrived with a coat of arms embossed on the envelope.

Elsie caught George squinting at it on the console table in the hall, while she sorted out the letters that she thought it safe to let Mother see.

"Do you think that's from the Bart?" George said. "*He* won't be asking us for money."

"Don't bet on it," Elsie said. "If he only inherited the title he may be as hard-up as we were. Ten to one he's got a draughty castle and an attic full of ancient retainers."

"What are ancient retainers?"

"Servants who have been in the family since he was a boy and still call him Master Gilbert although his white whiskers have grown down to his knees – aged footmen, decaying butlers, his old Nanny. Every good family has an old Nanny."

As far back as George could remember they had only ever had cook-generals and sometimes not even that, just a girl to help with the cleaning.

"So," Elsie went on, evilly, "he'll have his eye on Mother's twenty thousand. I bet he's a bounder who preys on widows and orphans. You and I will have to be very firm with her, Porge."

The letter *was* from the baronet, Sir Gilbert Bassett-Milne. Like all the other letter-writers he offered his congratulations to Mother but said he was really writing to tell her how pleased he was to discover new relatives, especially as the kids seemed to be about the same age as his own two, and how would they all like to come for a visit? His address was Hern House, Chertsey.

"A subtle rogue," Elsie muttered. "What's the betting he has rented a princely pile for the weekend, just to fool us. Stand by to repel bounders."

But even Elsie had to admit that Sir Gilbert sounded very ordinary and friendly. "After all, he didn't mention *his* title or *our* money once," she said, and let Mother borrow her new pen with the gold nib and a sheet of the special cream-laid paper to write an answer to Sir Gilbert, but made her practise on the back of a begging letter first.

"That cream-laid costs two bob a packet," said Elsie.

Five days later they took the train down to Chertsey.

"Will they come and meet us?" George asked. That would be a wonderful start to the weekend, being met by aristocrats. He had spent most of his life taking the bus, or walking.

"In a stolen motor car with a bogus chauffeur," Elsie said, stunning in a new frock and a meringue of a hat. Several young gentlemen had turned to look at her on Waterloo Station.

"*Not* gentleman," Elsie said. "Gentlemen would simply raise their hats and walk wistfully on."

"What were they, then?"

"*Clerks*."

Outside the station at Chertsey was a pony chaise with a lady sitting in it and a boy

standing by it with a tall, beautiful golden collie dog. As soon as the boy saw them he shouted, "There they are!" and ran forward, while the lady stepped down from the chaise and the dog danced on his hind legs.

"I'm Frederick Bassett-Milne," the boy said. He raised his cap to Mother and Elsie and winked at George. "This is Sabre, our faithful hound, and this is my mother – *down*, Sabre! – my mother, Lady Lil. How do you do?"

"Stow it, Fred," his mother said. "Take no

notice of him," she added to Mother. "None of us has got used to the title yet, except Bertie, and he's always behaved like Lord Muck anyway. You must be Mary Bassett, and Elsie . . . George. How nice to meet you."

Everyone was smiling and shaking hands, even Elsie. She had fallen in love with Lady Lil on sight. So had George. He later discovered that everyone did, but now they were all climbing into the chaise, and Fred was loading the luggage.

"I'll drive," he said. "George, you sit up in front, with me."

George hopped up beside Fred and the pony sauntered away from the station. It was not the kind of animal that George had expected a baronet to keep, but perhaps he had high-stepping Arabs in the stables.

On the other hand, Sabre, gambolling alongside, was a very noble-looking dog, with his flowing lion's mane and Roman nose.

While George was wondering how to talk to a member of the aristocracy, Fred solved the problem by speaking at high speed, just like anyone else.

" . . . and Mum says if she'd known she was going to be a lady she'd never have called herself Lily."

"Why did she have to call herself anything?" George said. "Didn't she have a name?"

"Lily de Lysle, her stage name. She was born

Doris Endicott, but, really, Doris wouldn't have sounded right for an actress, although Lady Doris sounds all right, but she could have been a Duchess. You know, a Duke proposed to her *five* times, twice in Hyde Park, once at the stage door, once at Henley Regatta and once at his ducal mansion, but she turned him down. Doris the Duchess, that would have been something. But Dad was just a humble artist. He kept quiet about there being a baronet in the family in case it put her off."

"Your mother was an actress?" George had never seen any actresses, on stage or off it, but he had thought that they were fast women with painted faces. Perhaps Sir Gilbert was really an actor and the whole thing was a fiendish hoax as Elsie had suspected – or pretended to suspect.

"Oh, yes," Fred said cheerfully. "That's why Sir Gervase cut Dad off without a shilling, for marrying her – and for becoming a painter when he was supposed to go into the army and lead his men to glory. You know the kind of thing. 'Out, Sirrah, and never darken my door again.' But no one could stop him inheriting the title. We're not after your money," he added hastily, turning red, and George turned just as red on Elsie's behalf. How could they have thought such a thing about these nice people? An actress and an artist for parents. Lucky, lucky Fred.

George had imagined that a baronet's home would be huge, turreted, moated, with battlements and perhaps a drawbridge, but it was just a low, red-brick house with a mossy-tiled roof, standing in a long garden with trees behind it and a sloping lawn, as big as a meadow, round three sides. Fred drove the chaise up to the front door and as they all climbed out a man appeared on the steps.

When they saw him Mother and Elsie stopped and gasped. George just stared. Sir Gilbert Bassett-Milne was tall and fair-haired. He had a neat beard and a cheerful moustache.

As soon as George saw him something clicked in his head. He could have sworn he actually heard the click, and at last he recognized the face that he thought he would never remember. There was no doubt at all, Sir Gilbert looked just like his own father; he really was a relative, and George suddenly felt enormously happy to think that this friendly man, and Fred, and lovely Lady Lil were part of his family.

"Tea, first," the baronet said, shaking hands and beaming. "Come in, drop everything, and *eat*."

Where were the ancient retainers? Tea was eaten in a fern-filled conservatory behind the house, and a maid brought out the tea things, but George saw no sign of the servants he had been expecting.

"Have you got a butler?" he whispered to Fred. Lady Lil heard him.

"We ought to have laid on a butler," she said, "to prove we have means." She turned to the

 baronet. "I've spent the whole journey from the station listening to our appalling son reveal the frightful family history and explain that we don't plan to embezzle Mary's inheritance." Watching Lady Lil during tea, George could understand what a good actress she must have been. Not that she was acting now, pretending to be someone she was not, but she knew how to make everyone have a good time, just by being there, with a voice that made you want to listen when she spoke and then wish that she would speak again.

All through the meal Sabre raced back and forth across the lawn, like a galloping golden thoroughbred, stopping now and again to sidle indoors and steal a cake. No one minded. No one seemed to mind about anything.

"Now, on the subject of dinner," Sir Gilbert said, before the maid had even carried away the tea trays, "we've some good friends joining us, but all are extremely ancient persons over the age of twenty-one. George, Fred, do you want to put on stiff collars and spend the evening listening to boring grown-ups or would you rather rampage around on your own and picnic in the playroom? No, hold your jaw, Fred. George is the guest, let him choose."

George knew exactly what Fred had been going to say so he said it instead. "Rampage and picnic please, Sir Gilbert."

"Oh, drop the Sir, do," the baronet said. "No one should be a Sir before he's fifty unless he's a Knight of the Round Table."

"What's Bertie going to do?" Fred asked. George had forgotten about Bertie, who must be Sir Gilbert's other son, Fred's brother, whose own mother had called him Lord Muck. But Sir Gilbert had written, *Your kids seem to be the same age as my two*. Well, Fred was certainly his age, so . . .

"Bertie is sure to go for the stiff collar and boredom," Lady Lil said, and at the moment the sun went in, just for a second or two, behind a small cloud, out of the trees stepped a tall figure, strolling across the grass towards them.

"Why," said Sir Gilbert, "there's Bertie now."

Chapter 3

"Hah d'you do?" Bertie said languidly, when he stepped indoors. He did not shake hands. Instead, he bowed to Mother and Elsie. He took no notice at all of Fred and George.

The sun had come out again, birds were singing, but in the conservatory there seemed to be a little patch of cooler, duller air around the tea party that dimmed even the glow of Lady Lil.

"Will you have some tea, Bertie?" she said, taking up a cup and saucer that had been set aside for him.

"No, I won't take

tea, thank you, Mother," he said stiffly, as if he was talking to a stranger.

"Cake?" Sir Gilbert held out the plate.

"No, thank you."

Everyone seemed to be on their best behaviour in Bertie's presence, even his parents. He had squashed the conversation dead, just by being there. People were speaking more quietly, either waiting for him to sit down or better still, George thought, to go away again.

George looked at him cautiously, in case Bertie turned suddenly and knew he was being watched.

Bertie was tall and fair, like his father, like George's father, but even though Bertie had no beard George could see that he didn't look much like either of them. Sir Gilbert and the man in the photograph on the piano at home had eyes made small by smiling, with lines in the corners. Bertie's eyes were large and round and strangely flat, like eyes in a painting. He had smiled once, when he bowed to Mother, but the smile had gone nowhere near his eyes.

How old was he? Sir Gilbert had hinted that he was Elsie's age. He looked younger than Elsie whose mouth and nose had grown thin and sharp with difficulty and disappointment, but he behaved in a way that made him seem much older. George could not imagine Bertie crying, "Oh, my eye!" the way Elsie did.

"Finished your fodder?" he asked, looking down on George and Fred. "I'll take them off your hands for a while," he said to his mother. "Come along, kids."

Who are you calling a kid? George thought. And no one wants us taken off their hands.

But no one seemed to want to argue with Bertie, either.

"I said, come along," Bertie commanded. "I'll give you a tour of the ancestral home. Time you got acquainted with your forebears, young Bassett."

George had been looking forward to exploring the house and garden with Fred. He had been sure that Fred would want to show him around when tea was finished. He was not at all sure what Bertie wanted but he was glad that Fred was coming with them.

He had seen only a little of the house as they came through on the way to the conservatory. It had looked very nice, although any house looked nice compared to his own, but it had not seemed the kind of place that needed a guided tour.

"Did you inherit it from Sir Gervase?" he asked Fred, but it was Bertie who answered.

"It's been in the family for generations," said Bertie, implying that the Bassett-Milnes had no need of wills and long-lost relatives. He led the way across the hall and reached out to close a door that was standing ajar. George just had time to glimpse a big, bright room lit by tall uncurtained windows.

"What's in there?" he asked, before realizing that Bertie had closed the door because he did not want George to see what lay behind it.

"Dad's studio," Fred said. "Where he paints."

"What sort of things does he paint?"

"The sort of pictures that *people* like," Bertie said. People, evidently, did not include Bertie.

"Can I see them?"

"I dare say he'll show you himself, soon enough," Bertie said, as if the paintings were a shameful secret that the family was trying to hush up.

There were other doors, but George dared not ask where they led, for Bertie was steering him past them with the back of George's collar pinched tight between thumb and forefinger.

George was not used to being hauled around like this. "I say, Bertie—" He tried to pull away, but Bertie simply let go of his collar to tweak his ear, with a painful nip.

"*You* call me Bertram," he said, fixing George with his flat, unfriendly eyes. "Only my friends and family call me Bertie."

"But I am your family," George said.

"*Are* you?" Bertie said. "Are you really?

Well, I'll tell you something, young Bassett. You may wish you weren't." He turned round suddenly. "Fred, you cut along and clean my cricket boots. And mind you do it properly this time."

"Yes, Bertie," Fred said meekly.

"I'll come and help," George said, but Bertie's hand was on his shoulder again.

"No, you don't," he said. "I've got something to show you. You and Fred can racket around later."

Fred disappeared through a green baize-covered door at the end of the hall. Bertie was steering George towards the staircase. It was wide and shallow, with polished wood, so unlike the steep flights at home with the hairpin bend in the middle and the dark alcove.

The landing ran the length of the house and had no windows, but Bertie touched a switch at the head of the stairs and the whole corridor lit up as if the sun had risen. Hern House had electric light!

"This is what we inherited," Bertie said. "If anything goes with the title, these do."

Along one wall was a row of paintings in

heavy frames that George thought must be solid gold until he looked closely. The paintings were portraits. The first one reminded George of the *Laughing Cavalier*; they had a print of it at home and he had always liked it because the Cavalier had the same cheerful moustache as the one in the photograph of Father, on the piano. And here it was again, on a big, fair, smiling man in a great black plumed hat with a lot of lace around his collar.

"Sir Andrew Bassett," Bertie said. "The first baronet. And this is his wife – Lady Margery."

The Bassett baronets and their wives stretched all the way down the corridor; Sir William and Lady Eleanor, Sir Humphrey and Lady Susan, Sir Robert and Lady Isabella. After that they became Bassett-Milnes; Sir Richard and Lady Jane, Sir James and Lady Caroline, Sir Gervase – who looked just as crabby as George had thought he would – and Lady Agatha who looked as if she had a lot to put up with.

"Who'll come next?" George said, "after Sir Gilbert, I mean."

"I shall," said Bertie. "Sir Bertram, the ninth baronet." And George remembered what Lady Lil had said: "Bertie's always behaved like Lord Muck."

"Was Sir Gervase your grandfather?" George

said. There were so many ancestors, he was losing track of them. And was being a Bassett-Milne grander than being a mere Bassett?

"Great-grandfather," Bertie said.

"What happened to *his* son?"

"The Shadow of the Bassetts," Bertie said. He lowered his voice. "Never once, since the baronetcy was founded in 1661, has an eldest son lived to inherit the title."

"What happens to them?"

"They are . . . shadowed," Bertie said. "While they are young they are stupid and carefree, like all kids are, but as each one becomes a man the shadow grows up with him and follows him wherever he goes. And enters his heart. And steals his soul away."

They had reached the top of the stairs again, and on those words Bertie touched the electric light switch, plunging the landing into eerie dusk. "They die in a state of *morbid dread*."

He was whispering now. George had to strain to hear what he was saying.

"Was your father an eldest son?" Bertie murmured.

"Yes, but he wasn't heir to the title."

"Any eldest son can be heir to the title," Bertie said meaningfully.

"Yes, but—"

"But?"

"He died of fever."

"No one ever tells little kids the truth," Bertie said.

"My mother wouldn't lie to me," George said.

"I suppose she didn't want to upset you."

"You take it back! My mother never lies."

"I didn't say she lied," Bertie said, smoothly soothing. "But it's not something *we* ever talk about – so don't go blabbing to the others. I should keep quiet about it, if I were you," he went on. "I mean, you're an eldest son, aren't you?"

"So are you," George said fiercely.

"You're making this up. You're just trying to frighten me."

"Oh, no," Bertie said. "I'm not an eldest son."

"Then you won't be the ninth baronet, will you? It's all made-up lies."

"Yes, I shall," Bertie said smugly. "I shall be the ninth baronet and *you* will have a shadow. That's what you get for being a Bassett and an eldest son."

Bertie was not touching George now. There was nothing to stop George turning his back and going down the stairs, but Bertie's flat, pale eyes seemed to hold him fast where he stood.

"Everyone's got a shadow," George said. "There's nothing in shadows."

"Just because you can't see anything," Bertie said, "it doesn't mean that there isn't anything to see." At last he looked away, and George raced downstairs to find Fred, in the sunlight, away from the shadows.

Chapter 4

Lady Lil had been right about Bertie, who dressed for dinner and joined the grown-ups downstairs. Fred and George lurked at the top to watch the guests arrive, and stayed to see everyone cross the hall into the dining

room. Mother, all shiny and smiling, talked and laughed with Lady Lil. Elsie was escorted by one of the guests, and George was sure he

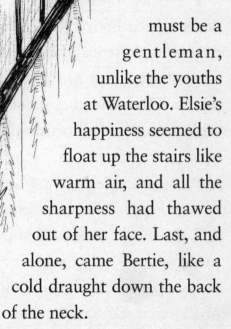

must be a gentleman, unlike the youths at Waterloo. Elsie's happiness seemed to float up the stairs like warm air, and all the sharpness had thawed out of her face. Last, and alone, came Bertie, like a cold draught down the back of the neck.

Fred's playroom was big and shabby and full of big, shabby

furniture that could no longer be used downstairs.

"It all comes up here so I can crash around and not have to worry about spoiling it," Fred explained. George wondered if Bertie shared the room with Fred, and crashed around. He thought not.

There were low cupboards all along the walls where Fred kept his books and model engines and ships and cricket gear – and one especially for his paints. George had a paintbox with two moulting brushes and most of the paint pans scoured out to get at the last little bit of  colour. Fred had sable brushes and tubes of oils and the whole cupboard smelled thrillingly of turpentine, like an exotic incense. There were piles of paper and sketchbooks on shelves, tubs of charcoal sticks and pencils, pens and bottles of ink and even a couple of canvasses leaning against the back of the cupboard.

"Are you going to be a painter too – like Sir Gilbert?" George said, tenderly stroking the silky sables. He used his paints only for colouring pictures in magazines when it was raining. This was serious stuff.

"I want to be a cricketer, but I don't suppose I could earn my living by it," Fred confessed. "Dad thinks I've got promise, though. He lets me work with him. Look here" – Fred blushed easily and he blushed now as he spoke – "he, Dad, asked me to have a word with you about . . . about, well, he said if you keep calling him Sir Gilbert he'll have to go out and slay a dragon. All his friends call him Gib, like they always did. Just say Uncle Gib – he'd like that. He's never been an uncle."

"Do you think he'd let me see his paintings? Can I look at yours?"

"Oh, you won't want to see *them*." Fred blushed again. George did want to see them but guessed that Fred was shy so he did not push him. "But just ask Dad in the morning,"

Fred went on. "He'd have offered to show you but he was afraid you'd say yes, just to be polite, and then be bored."

"I don't think Sir – your father – Uncle Gib – could *ever* be boring. Or your mother. She's awfully jolly. Ought I to call her Auntie?"

"No, Lady Lil will do. She thinks it's funny. That's what everyone calls her."

"Well, I think you're all A1," George said. Except Bertie, he added silently. Bertie was like no one else in this wonderful family – but there was more to the family than George knew about. There was Sir Gervase for a start. He might have been just like Bertie, cutting relatives out of his will the way that Bertie seemed to want to cut George out of his family. Could all that rot about eldest sons be true? George wanted to ask Fred but didn't like to risk it. Suppose it *was* true. Bertie had said it was something they never talked about. It would be awful if it did turn out to be true and he upset everyone by mentioning it.

They had dinner on the hearthrug, turning out the light and pretending that they were sitting by a campfire in the heart of the bush.

Sounds of conversation drifted up from the party downstairs and whenever there was a burst of laughter Fred hissed, "'ware lions," or "The wildebeest are restless tonight." One of the ladies had a high, swooping giggle. "It is the hunting cry of the wily hyena." George said, and felt very proud of his wit when Fred fell over laughing.

Fred's bedroom opened out of the playroom

and George was in a spare room, next but one from that, along the landing.

"Pity we're not next door to each other," Fred said. "We could tap coded messages on the wall. Still, next time you can come in with me. Mum thought we'd better not bunk together first time in case we didn't get on."

George felt sorry that he was staying for only one night, but Fred had said, "Next time". Of course there would be a next time.

"Who's in between us?" George asked as they parted in the corridor after Fred had shown him where the bathroom was.

"Bertie," said Fred, and there was no need for him to say anything else. No one would be tapping coded messages on Bertie's wall.

The bathroom was A1 too, with hot water from a glorious roaring geyser that looked as if it might take off through the ceiling like a rocket. But when George opened the door to go back to his room he found the corridor outside in darkness, lit only by a flickering candle that glided towards him held in an unseen hand.

George was used to candlelight. They had often used candles at home in the old days, especially when the gas bill was due. He had never liked it because it was a sign of bad things to come, and he liked it even less now. Candlelight made darkness darker, it made shadows shift, and from somewhere in those shadows a voice said, "That's right, young Bassett. Off to bed. You must be tired after all that *climbing*."

Bertie's face, lit from below, sneered at him over the candle like a gargoyle.

"Climbing?" George said. He could think only of the mountaineering game that he and Fred had played after dinner, propping one sofa against another and ascending the Matterhorn, with toasting forks.

"Haven't you heard of *social* climbing?" Bertie said. "People from families like *yours*, trying to get in with families like *ours*. You can't buy your way into decent people's books."

George could think of several answers to that because both families obviously liked each other very much – except for Bertie. But as he was only a guest in Bertie's house he said nothing.

"Holding your tongue? Very wise," Bertie said. "I suppose you've been blabbing to young Fred about the Shadow of the Bassetts? You look like a sneak – your kind always are."

"No, I haven't," George said. "I forgot all about it." That was true. He and Fred had had such a good time there had been no chance to remember Bertie's sinister hints.

"I wouldn't forget if I were you," Bertie said. "Come here, I want to show you something."

The flame flared smokily as it floated along the corridor, past the ancestors to the painting of the very first baronet. Bertie held the candle up to Sir Andrew's face.

"See?" Bertie said.

"See what?"

"Behind him."

The whole of the portrait's background was dim.

"It's only paint."

"*Just* behind him."

Was it the candle's flicker that showed a darker darkness behind Sir Andrew, or was there something . . . ?

"The Shadow," Bertie said. "The Shadow of the Bassetts. The artist saw it and painted it in."

A voice from below called out, "I say, Bertie! Are you ever coming back?"

"One day," Bertie said, "I'll tell you how Sir Andrew got his shadow, and why it haunts the Bassetts to this day."

Then he shoved the candlestick into George's hand and ran lightly down to the hall.

"Sleep well," cried Bertie, from the foot of the stairs.

The ancestors leered and winked in the candlelight as George groped his way back to his room. Was that a shadow at Sir Humprey's back, a shadow looming over the shoulder of Sir Richard, or was it just the way they were painted? No, they would have no shadows. They were not eldest sons. If they had been eldest sons they would not have lived to become baronets.

George's own shadow, the shadow of an eldest son, followed him into his room and swooped across the wall until he switched on the light and snuffed the candle. His room was small, four-square and bright under the electric bulb, but the trouble with electric light, he discovered, was that when you turned it off it was right off. He could not turn it down like the gas lamps at home, and then the room was very, very dark.

George thought of lighting the candle again,

but the candle would cast shadows. Instead
he made a cave under the bed-
clothes and burrowed
into it, just as he used to
do when he was small
and afraid of the dark.

It had been a wonderful
day, a wonderful evening.
Why did Bertie have to come and spoil it with
his tales of heirs and shadows? It was all rot,
anyway.

Wasn't it?

Still, he thought, Fred likes me. Fred's my
friend. Fred will be my friend for ever.

Fred seemed to think so too. The Bassetts
were going home after lunch, but first of all
Fred beckoned George into a quiet place
behind the conservatory and brought out a
beautiful little knife with a horn handle and
folding blades.

"Let's make a vow," he said, and with the

54

smallest blade he cut a little slit in the ball of his thumb. Then he passed the knife over for George to do the same, and they pressed the wounds together.

"Now we're blood brothers," Fred said. "I mean, I know we're only three-quarters cousins or something, but we promise to be blood brothers and swear always to defend each other and never let the other fellow down."

They swore, solemnly, and as they stopped speaking Bertie's voice said, "Dirty little beasts."

Bertie was standing in the doorway of the conservatory. "Fred, Mother wants you," he said. "She's in the drawing room – no, you stay here, young Bassett. I had something to tell you, didn't I?"

Fred went off reluctantly, sucking his thumb. George wanted to suck his, it was sore, but not with Bertie watching.

"Let's take a turn around the lawn," Bertie

said. They walked away from the house and George looked back towards the windows of the room where Mother and Uncle Gib and Elsie and Lady Lil were drinking coffee. Someone waved, he saw a hand, but he did not know whose. If only he could be in there now, with Fred.

"In fact," Bertie was saying, "I'm the eldest son *now* – the elder son, actually – but I wasn't the first-born. Father and Mother had a son before me but he died in infancy. We never talk about him."

"What was his name?" George asked. This seemed to throw Bertie. He paused.

"Arthur," he said finally. "Really, when I said the Shadow of the Bassetts falls upon the eldest son, I should have said, on the first-born. Like the tenth plague of Egypt."

"What?"

"Don't you know your Bible, you ignorant toad? When Pharaoh wouldn't let the Children of Israel leave Egypt, God sent ten plagues to smite him. And the last, the *worst*, the one that made Pharaoh change his mind, was the death of the first-born son. Every first-born son."

"I remember," George said. "Wasn't there a plague of frogs as well? Do Bassetts get plagued by frogs?"

"You stupid little beast." Bertie's face, full of rage, was suddenly very close to George's own. "Think what it's like to live all your life with a shadow at your back, waiting to get you, knowing it's there, wondering when it will strike. Think about it. Because you'll know how it feels soon enough."

Chapter 5

There was just time, after lunch, to do something to please Uncle Gib.

"Fred says you might let me look at your paintings," George said. "I'd like to, awfully, if you don't mind."

"I thought you'd never ask," Uncle Gib said, and took George into the studio which smelled of turpentine, like Fred's cupboard. There was a half-finished painting on an easel – so half finished that George could not quite guess at how it might turn out when it *was* finished, and many others, hanging on the wall or stacked against it, all full of light and movement, quite unlike the stiff dark portraits on the landing.

There were two of Lady Lil and several of Fred, all done out-of-doors, dappled with sunlight; Fred with the pony, Fred with Sabre, Fred with his bicycle. Close to, they did not look like anything at all, but Uncle Gib made George stand at a certain distance and then he could see them clear as anything, so alive and bright he could swear that Lady Lil smiled at him, that Sabre's golden mane rippled in the breeze and little leaf shadows moved on the wall.

"Oh, they're ripping," George exclaimed. "All of them."

There were no pictures of Bertie.

"Next time you come you'll have to sit for me," Uncle Gib said. "Don't worry, I never make people sit for too long or they start to look stuffed. Do you think Elsie would care to have her likeness limned? I mean, would she let me paint her portrait?"

"Oh, she'd love it," George said. "Do you paint everyone?"

"Everyone I can catch," Uncle Gib said.

"Except Bertie. Bertie doesn't care for my style of painting. He prefers the Pre-Raphaelites."

"What are they?"

"Wounded knights, beleaguered maidens, abandoned brides in moated mansions, lovers parting for ever at sunset and people dying of consumption."

George thought that sounded a lot like Bertie.

Before they left, Lady Lil lined them all up outside the front door and took a photograph. George stood next to Mother. For a second, just as Lady Lil pressed the shutter release, he could have sworn he felt a chill shadow at his back, but when he looked around it was only Bertie, standing behind them.

"Well," said Elsie, when they were on the train heading back to London, "that was something. I'd rather have them than the money. Mind you, I can only say that because we *have* got the money."

"Don't be vulgar," Mother tutted.

"Oh, don't be so Victorian," Elsie cried, but then they laughed because they had both had such a good time.

"We'll see them again soon, won't we?" George said.

"Not half," said Elsie, vulgar as anything.

"What did you think of Bertie?" George asked her later, when they were home.

"Who?"

"Bertie – Bertram – the older brother."

"Ghastly child," Elsie said.

"Child? I thought Sir – Uncle Gib said he was your age."

"He said *about* my age. He was guessing, he didn't know us then. Bertie's only fourteen."

"Fourteen?" No wonder seventeen-year-old Elsie had scarcely noticed him, except as a ghastly child.

"Why ghastly?"

"The way he behaves you'd think he was the ninth baronet already. You didn't see him at dinner, yaw-yawing and haw-hawing. In ten years" time he'll bore for England."

George felt cheered by Elsie's contempt, but going up to bed that evening he found himself looking nervously at that shad-  owed place on the bend of the stairs. It was weeks now since the builders had stopped the damp in the room on the half landing. The door was no longer locked and Mother had turned it into a sewing room. He knew what lay on the other side of the door, but he still heard Bertie's silken voice over his shoulder as he climbed the stairs.

"Just because you can't see anything, it doesn't mean that there isn't anything to see."

Then the photograph arrived, with a note from Lady Lil asking when they would be making their next, longer visit. The photograph joined the others on top of the piano and George looked at it often. Uncle Gib was sitting in the middle with Mother on his right and Elsie on his left. Fred stood by Elsie and George by Mother and behind George was Bertie. At first George thought Bertie must have moved just as the photograph was taken, but George had seen photographs like

that before. If people moved they looked fuzzy, smeary, with all their features run together. Bertie just looked as if someone had drawn a thick line down one side of him – a dark line, like when you stood close to your own shadow on the wall. But there was nothing behind Bertie except the front of the house, yards away, and in any case the sun was not shining in that direction. George decided it must be a trick of the light or a fault on the film.

A week after that George received a letter all of his own, with just his name on the envelope. It was from Fred.

We had such a jolly time, Mum says why don't you come on your own for the weekend before we go back to school?

Fred had drawn a picture of his school, and a cartoon of the headmaster. At least, George hoped it was a cartoon. Supposing teachers really looked like that? Fred might be going *back* to school but George was starting at his, Dr Mason's in Archway Road, his first school ever. He was not entirely looking forward to it and was ready to promise Mother anything if she would let him go to Hern House first. Mother just smiled – she smiled all the time, these days – and said of course he should go. Lady Lil had written as well, to make it official.

He went on his own, by train, and raced out of the station expecting to find Fred waiting with the pony chaise.

There was the chaise, but sitting in the driver's seat was Bertie.

"Well, young Bassett," Bertie said, staring down at him.

Ghastly child. He's only fourteen, George reminded himself. But fourteen was a lot older than George.

"Where's Fred?"

"Cut his stupid knee, playing around like a stupid kid," Bertie said hatefully. "They had to get the doctor to look at it. So he won't be playing any kiddie games with you, young Bassett. Never mind," he added. "I'll entertain you instead. Up you come."

He leaned down and held out his hand, but as George reached out to take it, Bertie seemed to start and made a wild grab at nothing, so that George slipped and banged his own knee against the wheel.

"What's the matter?"

Bertie was staring somewhere over Georgie's shoulder. "Strange," he said.

"What's strange?" George climbed up carefully, without Bertie's help.

"You weren't where I thought you would be."

"Yes, I was."

"I could have sworn . . ." Bertie shook his head and rubbed his eyes. ". . . something behind you. Perhaps it was a trick of the light. Perhaps it was your shadow."

You need your eyes tested, George thought, but he did not say it. He was going to be with Bertie for twenty minutes on the drive to Hern House.

It was rather less than twenty minutes this time. The pony did not amble with Bertie at the reins. Bertie drove as if he were racing four-in-hand. When the roof of Hern House appeared above the trees, Bertie slowed down.

"Now, listen, young Bassett," he said, "don't think I can't see what you're playing at."

"I'm not playing," George said.

"Not just you, your family. You're not the

67

sort of people we know, so don't go thinking it. Don't go thinking you can come here exactly when you like. You're not one of us. You never will be. None of you will."

"You've no right to say that about Mother. Lady Lil—"

"*Don't dare to call her that*," Bertie snarled. "And don't call my father Uncle Gib. He's not your uncle."

"Well, what do I call them?" George asked. Bertie had not thought of that, but before

 he could come up with an answer, Uncle Gib himself overtook them on a bicycle, waving and smiling, with Sabre prancing at his side.

"You can call him *Sir*, you little guttersnipe," Bertie hissed.

"And if I hear you address my mother as Lady Lil, I'll give you such a licking you'll have to *crawl* back to Hornsey."

Chapter 6

Fred was in the studio with his leg propped up on a stool.

"Captive model," Uncle Gib said. "He can't get away. Sit next to him, George, and we'll have a double portrait."

George perched on a stool beside Fred, and Uncle Gib disappeared behind the easel. They could see his left hand with a fist full of charcoal sticks, and every few moments his face looked round the side of the canvas he was working on.

"Rotten luck getting crocked like that," George said.

"Rotten luck for *you*. I was going to show

you the river – there's good fishing under the bridge. I expect I'll be able to hobble around after lunch a bit. We can go to the gazebo."

"Button your lip for thirty seconds, Fred, there's a good chap," Uncle Gib said.

"But, Dad, you always say you like to capture freedom of movement."

"There are limits. Your jaw is going up and down like a threshing machine."

George could not imagine what a gazebo was. It sounded as if it might be a sort of zoo, or some kind of animal that lived in one, but after lunch Fred, limping professionally with a gnarled stick for support, led him across the lawn, round the trees to a white-painted summer house with lattice-work walls.

"Why's it called a gazebo?" George said.

"Never thought. Perhaps it's because you can *gaze* out of it," Fred said.

Fred kept emergency rations in the gazebo – chocolate bars and stone bottles of ginger beer. It was sheltered in the white-domed room with the trees around it, although out in the garden the wind was blowing quite hard and cloud shadows blinked across the grass and over the house. But when Bertie appeared it was not from the direction of the house. He suddenly loomed up in the doorway.

Fred had his back to Bertie and did not see him arrive. He was in the middle of a story about a cricket match at his school. George paid close attention. Soon, he thought, he would be playing cricket at school – well, perhaps not at Dr Mason's, but soon, when he was old enough, when he went on to Anderton College, Father's old school, something which three months ago he had never dreamed would happen.

71

"Stop bragging, Fred," Bertie said, and they both jumped. "Decent people don't – but you wouldn't know about that, would you, young Bassett?"

Fred didn't understand what Bertie meant, but George did.

"Where's the other fellow?" Bertie said.

"What other fellow?" Fred looked all round.

"Where's he gone?"

"There's no one here but us," George said.

"Really? When I came out of the trees I could have sworn there were three of you in here." Bertie looked under the benches and round the back of the gazebo. "Strange. There were definitely three people unless" – he looked at George – "it was a trick of the light."

"Probably a shadow," Fred said innocently.

"Oh, yes, that must have been it. A shadow. Mustn't it, young Bassett? It was right beside you."

Bertie turned away and began to walk back towards the house.

"I say, he does come out with the rummiest things," Fred said. "Look, there's a bit of choc left. Let's break it in half."

George was watching  Bertie. An extra-large cloud was passing and although there was sunlight on the fields beyond Hern House, none fell upon the lawn, and yet George was sure that Bertie trailed a shadow behind him across the grass; if not a shadow, something dark that went where Bertie went.

George wanted to say, "Do you *like* your brother?" but probably Fred did like him, even if he wouldn't admit to it in public. He wanted to ask, "Do you know anything about your other brother, Arthur, the one who died before you were born?" But Bertie had said they never talked about that, and Fred might be hurt by the question, even though he and George were blood brothers and pledged to stand by each other and never let the other fellow down.

That had been Fred's idea. George did not want him to wish that it hadn't been.

They did not see much of Bertie after that, but he was there at dinner. Because there were no grown-up guests this time the boys ate downstairs with Uncle Gib and Lady Lil. Bertie sat opposite George. Every time George looked across at Bertie, Bertie was looking at him – no, not *at* him . . .

At first he looked at him and then immediately looked away again, as if George was not there, or not worth the bother. But after a while, George noticed, Bertie began to stare, not at George but at something over George's left shoulder. He would poke his head forward a little, as if to see better, and then blink and shake his head. It was done very subtly. No one else seemed to notice.

And then at last Bertie would look directly at George, and smile sadly.

Each time, it was all George could do not to

look round too, and in the end he did – and saw his reflection in the window and Bertie's reflection staring back at him.

"Is it getting chilly?" Lady Lil asked him. "It seemed so mild for April – but do close the window if you like."

"Chilly . . . no," George said, but suddenly he was feeling chilly and it was not because of the open window.

"Only, you keep looking round."

"Strange," Bertie said softly. "That feeling that there's something behind you."

It was Bertie who was behind George later as he went along the corridor from the bathroom. He knew it was Bertie even before he looked round, and started to move faster, but Bertie overtook him.

"What's the hurry, young Bassett?" Bertie said. "Do wait a moment. I was going to tell you something, wasn't I?"

"You're always telling me things," George

said. He did not care what Bertie told him now. Tonight he was sharing Fred's room.

"About Sir Andrew," Bertie said. "Remember?"

They were beside the portrait of Sir Andrew and Sir Andrew's shadow. Sir Andrew looked remarkably pleased with himself for a doomed man.

"He was a base betrayer," Bertie said. "Not a nobleman, a common traitor. In the Civil War, when Englishman fought Englishman and brother fought brother, he was captain in Cromwell's New Model Army, but secretly he was a spy for the Royalists. After King Charles the First was beheaded he fled abroad and Cromwell cursed him with his dying breath. When Charles the Second came back from exile and took the throne he made the traitor Andrew Bassett a baronet – but the curse struck."

"What was the curse?"

"That his treacherous sin should shadow him all his days, and his son, and his son after him. Every first-born of the name of Bassett."

"But I'm not a first-born," George said. "Elsie is."

"Women don't count," Bertie snapped. "Women can't inherit titles. Women can't even *vote*. You're a first born *son*, aren't you? Aren't you? And you're a *nobody*, like him." He stabbed his finger towards the painting. "You're a Bassett. A nobody, from nowhere."

"Well, you're a Bassett too," George said. As Bertie grew angrier and angrier he seemed to feel calmer and calmer.

"*We* are Bassett-Milnes," Bertie said, clenching his fist. "Milnes sailed with Sir Francis Drake. Milnes fought beside Wellington at Waterloo!"

"Waterloo Station?" George said, and ducked under Bertie's arm, down the corridor and into the playroom where Fred was waiting.

Chapter 7

After that it was quite a while before any of them visited Hern House again. George started at Dr Mason's with a warning from Mother ringing in his ears.

"Darling, *don't* go telling people about legacies and having baronets in the family. It's so vulgar, boasting about one's connections."

"And anyway," Elsie put in brutally, "everyone knows we hadn't a bean this time last year. Just keep your rat-trap shut, Porge."

George had not dreamed of boasting about his connections and wished Mother had not mentioned it. It was too close to what Bertie had said about buying your way into decent people's society. But as it turned out, no one at school talked about their relatives. It was scarcely done even to admit that you had a mother.

Sometimes letters came from Fred, mainly about cricket and someone called Anstruther. *He's my best friend*, Fred wrote, and then, before George had time even to start feeling jealous, *You have to have a best friend at school, all the chaps do. But we are blood brothers for ever.*

George took the hint and palled up with a boy in his form called Wilkes, because he knew Fred was right. Having a blood brother was special, but Fred was miles away and a fellow did need someone at his side to fight off bullies and sneaks like Robson, who taunted George: "*Your* sister used to teach *my* sister music. Why did she leave The Manor? Did she have to leave? Was there a scandal?"

George and Wilkes dealt with Robson on the way home, under the railway arch.

One day Uncle Gib and Lady Lil came to tea after visiting some artist friends in Camden Town. Mother loved having people to tea these days. All the rooms were freshly painted, there were new curtains at every window and new carpets in the parlour and the hall.

"We've had orders from Fred," Lady Lil told George. "We are to have you ready and waiting when he comes home for the holidays, but would you mind awfully holding back a day or two, so we can at least have a look at him before you both disappear into the foothills of the Himalayas or the sands of the Kalahari?"

But on the day that George was due to go down to Hern House a telegram came. Telegrams nearly always meant bad news. People dreaded the little yellow envelopes, but they were the quickest way to get in touch if you had no telephone, and not many people did have, not even the eighth baronet, although Uncle Gib had talked of having one installed if he ever felt his friends were forgetting him.

"Fred has come home from school with measles," Mother said, when she had finally brought herself to open the telegram. "Three weeks' quarantine. What bad luck."

Fred sent a letter a few days later with *From my deathbed* written on the back, which was a sure sign that he was getting better, although the envelope had to be baked in the oven before George was allowed to open it, to get rid of the measle germs.

Fred's news made George even more disappointed than he was already. *Bertie's gone on a boating hol with some school friends*, he wrote, *so I'm all alone here. Sickening luck*. Fred, as he often did, had drawn pictures round his letter. George could see that Fred really did have promise as an artist, but this time the drawings did not cheer him up much, even though one of them was of Bertie falling out of a boat into Iffley Lock, at Oxford.

Hern House without Bertie oiling around it would have been heaven. During the term George had mainly forgotten about Bertie, especially as home was now so well lit and it grew dark so late in summer. Even so, he could never quite forget about the shadow – not the shadow that once lurked on the staircase but the one that Bertie had told him about.

It was never there at school, there was no time for it, but often he had the sensation that something was behind him. He seemed to need to look over his shoulder a lot these days, and sometimes, for no reason at all, he felt the short hairs on the back of his neck bristle and a creeping feeling, lower down, just below his collar. He woke in the night more often and was sure that he heard a soft rustling somewhere in the bedroom. He never saw anything but, "Just because you can't see anything," Bertie had said, "it doesn't mean that there isn't anything to see."

Elsie was out a lot, with new friends. She had started studying music again, and went to concerts and the theatre. Once, George had known she was there at night, on the far side of the wall. Now he could not be certain, and he was far too old to say, "I don't want to go to bed before Elsie comes home."

In any case, to say that would be to admit that he believed in the shadow that lay in wait for him – for all the first-born sons who bore the Bassett name. In the daylight George was pretty sure that if a shadow haunted him it was the thought of Bertie himself, with his cold flat eyes and chilly contempt. Bertie was enough to make anyone's hair stand on end.

*

At last, word came from Hern House. Fred was out and about again. He came with Uncle Gib to collect George and they all went down to Chertsey together.

And there, when they arrived, was Bertie, home from his holiday; Bertie, who thought George was not good enough to be part of his family and would do anything to frighten him out of it. Then George remembered the shadow all over again – remembered that he was a first-born son.

At dinner, he was glad to see that he was not sitting opposite Bertie, but then he realized that Bertie would be sitting next to him instead. Everyone was in a good mood, laughing and talking and toasting Fred's recovery. Bertie said very little, but now and again George caught him glancing down behind George's chair.

"I thought I saw something," Bertie murmured, "just for a second. Must be a trick of the light."

In the end George said, "Why can't anyone else see it, then?"

"No one else is looking," Bertie purred.

Rushing around the house and garden with Fred and Sabre, George knew it was all nonsense.

When they sat in Uncle Gib's airy studio while he painted them, George knew it was all nonsense. They were often out all day, fishing or exploring. Nonsense, it was all nonsense.

Fred had a bicycle. Lady Lil fetched Bertie's old machine from an outhouse.

"This ought to fit you for now," she said. Unfortunately while Fred was helping George to practise in the lane, Bertie came round the corner.

George braked to avoid running into him and Bertie seized the handlebars.

"*Who* said you could ride that?" he asked in his quietest voice.

"Lady— your mother. I'm only borrowing it."

Bertie could not argue with that but he looked over George's left shoulder and narrowed his eyes.

"I wouldn't go racing around on it if I were you," he said.

"Remember what happens to first-born Bassetts. You aren't on your own, you know."

"No, I'm with Fred," George said, but Bertie just smiled lazily.

As he rode away, George could not help looking back and wobbled out of control, so that his back wheel tangled with Fred's front wheel and they both fell off. By this time Bertie was nowhere to be seen.

Later, when they were having tea in the play-room, because it had started raining, George said, "Does Bertie ever tell you stories?"

"*Lies?*" Fred said. George was always afraid of offending Fred by saying anything less than complimentary about Bertie. George and Fred might be blood brothers, but Fred and Bertie were brothers born. After all, George did not always feel very fond of Elsie, but he would hit any cad, like Robson, who insulted her.

"No, stories – ghost stories."

"Oh, no," Fred said. "He  thinks that kind of thing is the most awful rot. He doesn't even *read* stories, not any kind. Grandma used to send him loads of books – *Treasure Island* and *Kidnapped* and *The Gorilla Hunters* – all A1. He never even looked at them. I've got them now – you can borrow them if you like." He pointed to the shelves under the window. "He is an ass."

Ass was not the word George would have used. "What does he read, then?"

"Oh, stuff in Dad's library – history and science. School sorts of things."

Uncle Gib managed to pin them down for long enough to finish the portrait. As with all his others, it looked nothing like anything, close to, but from across the room you could see at once that it was George and Fred, even down to the kink in George's eyebrow from the scar where he had fallen over the coal scuttle on his third birthday. But up close he could not even find the eyebrow among those ridges and furrows of paint.

Lady Lil was delighted. "We'll get that framed and hung."

"With the baronets?" George asked.

"Not likely," said Lady Lil, who occasionally forgot to be a lady. "You don't want to skulk on the landing with those old horrors, do you? We only hung them at all out of respect for Sir Gervase, and we put them up there so we wouldn't have to see them too often. You and Fred can go in the drawing room, where everyone can see you all the time."

"Haven't they been in the family for generations – the portraits?" George asked.

"Not in *our* family," Lady Lil said. "They came with the title, like nightmares with lobster. Gib's afraid people will think he admires them, when he thinks they're the worst paintings he's seen. That's really why they went upstairs. It seems to run in the family – every baronet must have chosen the worst painter he could find, or the cheapest. You know, whoever painted the first one, what's his name – Sir Andrew – was a penny-pinching cheat. He didn't even use new canvas. If you catch it in a certain light you can see the outline of someone else underneath the background."

"Does Bertie know that?" George said it without meaning to.

"Bertie – oh, I should think so. Everyone knows about it."

Chapter 8

It was thundery next day. Even the studio seemed dim and the landing was a long dark tunnel, but Fred turned the electric light on and they practised slow bowling under the gaze of the seven baronets and their ladies.

George could see, plain as anything, the phantom figure beneath the painted background of Sir Andrew's portrait. Let Bertie try *that* one again, he thought and then jumped. A shadow was coming up the stairs.

It was Bertie. He looked at him disdainfully and went into his room. George stared after him. The light was on in the corridor but not in the hall downstairs. How could he have seen Bertie's shadow before he saw Bertie?

At dinner he and Fred were first in the dining room. George sat down and was about to ask Fred to sit next to him, but Fred had already gone to the place opposite. Although he felt at home in Hern House George did not feel so at home that he could start telling people where to sit, even Fred. Fred would not mind, but Lady Lil might be offended. He would be sitting next to Bertie again.

The others came in just then and George felt Bertie push unnecessarily against him as he went to sit down. He looked round, longing to shove back, but Bertie's chair was empty. At that moment, Bertie himself pushed past George and sat down. George gaped at him. Who was it who just a moment ago—?

"Don't try that trick on me, young Bassett,"

Bertie said, not even looking at him.

"What trick?"

"Looking for shadows behind *my* chair. Won't wash, young Bassett."

There was nothing behind Bertie's chair, but the air seemed very thick around him. George remembered the photograph that Lady Lil had taken at the end of that first visit – the strange dark outline at Bertie's side. If George glanced out of the tail of his eye, Bertie seemed to have it now. Perhaps it was a trick of the light.

At the end of the meal Bertie was the first to leave the table. As he went out of the door, George was almost certain that something went out with him. Why could no one else see? But Bertie had already supplied the answer to that: "No one else is looking."

Next morning George ran into Uncle Gib accidentally-on-purpose, as he was going into the studio.

"Uncle, can I ask you something?"

"Of course you can. Come in with me while I set up."

George sat on a stool to watch as Uncle Gib put on his smock and selected some tubes of paint to squeeze on to his palette. He stood a half-finished canvas on the easel.

"What are you painting today?"

"The Honourable Mrs Octavius Legge – due for a sitting at half-past ten. Curious name for a leg – Octavius. Mr and Mrs Leg. What are your legs called?"

"Sir Humphrey and Lady Susan," George said.

"That's right, keep it in the family. What did you want to ask me?"

George had been rehearsing. He did not want to tell even white lies to Uncle Gib, but he had to know. "One of the fellows at school, bit of a cad, really . . . said something about – about a family curse."

"His family?"

"No, ours. The curse of the first-born."

"What did he know about it?" Uncle Gib tapped his teeth with the end of a paintbrush. "Whatever he knows, it's more than I do."

"I think he'd read something in a book – how the eldest son never lives to inherit the title – that all the eldest sons in the family die young."

"How young? I'm an eldest son," Uncle Gib said. "I say, the curse might strike me down at any second, while I'm painting the Honourable Mrs Legge."

"I don't know what age," George said. "Is Bertie an eldest – elder son? First-born."

"I don't see any others, do you? Fred, as I recall, is three years younger."

"And there never – never were any others?" George hated saying it, perhaps reminding Uncle Gib, who he loved like a real uncle, of some tragedy he had bravely tried to forget.

"I think we'd have noticed another child," Uncle Gib said, cheerfully. "I'm sure my wife would have done. No, Bertie's the next baronet. Don't say you've been worrying about *him*, you chump. Save your sympathy, he's the hardest nut in the cluster. He never wastes his sympathy on anyone else. Bertie takes after the Milnes and they were all soldiers and pirates."

"*Pirates*," George said. "That'll be something to tell the chaps at school – having pirates in the family."

"Cold-blooded cut-throats," Uncle Gib said. "One of them sailed with Sir Francis Drake – and he was the biggest pirate of them all."

On the way out of the studio, George ran into a most elegant person in a hat the size of a sunshade, who had just handed her gloves and cape to Lady Lil. George recognized the hat from the canvas on Uncle Gib's easel.

"She thinks I'm the maid," said Lady Lil, who had come in from the garden wearing an apron. She had been cutting flowers.

"Huh, let her. She's only an honourable. You're a *real* lady," George said. "And do you mind if I call you Auntie, because I haven't got any aunts."

"I'm flattered, nephew," Lady Lil said, and because there was no one watching she gave him a kiss and he gave her one back. Lady Lil flung the Honourable Mrs Octavius Legge's

cape around her shoulders and swept down
the hall.

"Orf to the Opera," she said.

Later that day some friends drove over from
Windsor and asked if Bertie would care to go
back with them for a short visit. Bertie said
that he would.

"Keeping an eye on the kiddies all the time
is the most awful bore," he said.

George felt his heart leap; a few days without Bertie!

The friends stayed for tea and they ate in the garden, sitting on rugs on the grass and picnicking. Whenever George looked up he saw that Bertie was at his old game, staring over George's shoulder as if he could see something there.

Stare all you like, George thought. It won't wash. Hard nut, that's what you are. And a liar. And a snob. And a bully. You may not knock fellows about but you're still a bully and I hate you.

No, I don't, he thought, a minute or two later, and felt very grown up. I despise you. You can keep your stupid shadow.

After tea Bertie went and fetched his things and they all turned out to wave goodbye to the visitors. Already the sun seemed to be shining more brightly, as if something else were leaving the house with Bertie, as if all Bertie's bullying and lies and hateful secrets had gathered themselves together into one darkness that would cling and follow, wherever he went.

As the carriage bowled down the drive, Sabre bounded out of the shrubbery and flew across the lawn to run alongside, his shadow skimming the grass beside him. But George saw what at first he thought was another dog, or another shadow – a dark, low, smoky, snaky thing, on the far side of the drive, running neck and neck with Sabre.

At the end of the drive Sabre pulled up and danced on his hind legs, spinning and barking. The dark low thing seemed to spring up into the carriage, but it was a long way off now, and George could not be sure. Only, before, there had been three people in the carriage, and now, he was certain, there were four; Bertie and his friends and someone, something, else.

You can keep your stupid shadow, George had thought, and Bertie *was* keeping it.

Then the horses turned left, into the lane, and Sabre came back alone, with only his own shadow beside him, grinning happily and swinging his tail.

"I'll tell you what," Uncle Gib said. "Let's all go down to the coast for a day or two tomorrow. How would Folkestone suit you, Lily?"

"A1," Lady Lil said. "The boys can bathe, you can paint and I can lounge around with a parasol. Cycle down to the village at once and telegraph for rooms."

"Bertie hates the seaside," Fred said, as Uncle Gib sprinted towards the house.

"No, he doesn't," said his mother. "Bertie hates the sort of people who go to the seaside. He'll be much happier swanning around at Windsor. I'm going to pack. We leave at dawn!"

Fred turned cartwheels across the lawn. Sabre sailed through the air in pursuit of butterflies. George spread his arms and gazed up into the sky. It had never looked so blue, or the sun so golden. He felt as if he were in one of Uncle Gib's paintings, all air and light, and never a shadow to be seen.

Another book in the Shock Shop series ...

Hairy Bill
Susan Price

Something came down the chimney in Alex's
bedroom in the night – something that
paused and, in a Scottish accent, asked for
Mathesons. Alex thought he was dreaming.
But his mum's name is Matheson. And when
he goes downstairs the next morning,
something is clearly very wrong.

The house is unnaturally, indeed
frighteningly, tidy. Has there been a
break-in – by obsessively tidy thieves? Or is
there another, more sinister explanation?
Meet Hairy Bill – a supernatural, Scottish
whirlwind of terrifying tidiness.

Shock Shop titles available from Macmillan

The prices shown below are correct at the time of going to press. However, Macmillan Publishers reserve the right to show new retail prices on covers which may differ from those previously advertised.

Stealaway	K. M. Peyton	0 330 39739 7
Hairy Bill	Susan Price	0 330 93731 6
Long Lost	Jan Mark	0 330 39749 4
The Bodigulpa	Jenny Nimmo	0 330 39750 8
You Have Ghost-Mail	Terence Blacker	0 333 96001 7

All Macmillan titles can be ordered at your local bookshop or are available by post from:

Book Service by Post
PO Box 29, Douglas, Isle of Man IM99 1BQ

Credit cards accepted. For details:
Telephone: 01624 675137
Fax: 01624 670923
E-mail: bookshop@enterprise.net

Free postage and packing in the UK.
Overseas customers: add £1 per book (paperback)
and £3 per book (hardback)